This book belongs to

ELLA!

THANK you for READING
my book!

your friend,

CHEF NATHAN LYON

Sam The Clam

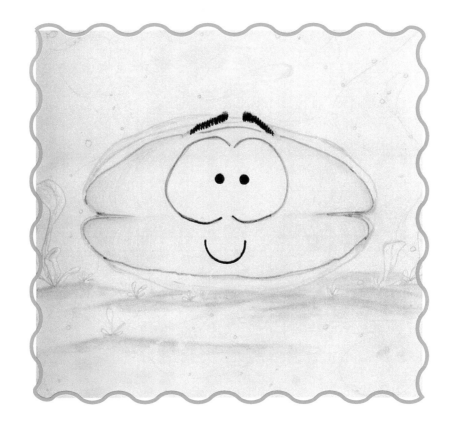

By Nathan W. Lyon

Illustrations by
Craig A. Lyon and Nathan W. Lyon

AuthorHouse™
1663 Liberty Drive
Bloomington, IN 47403
www.authorhouse.com
Phone: 1-800-839-8640

ISBN: 978-1-4520-7784-0 (sc)

First published by AuthorHouse 09/02/2010

Library of Congress Control Number: 2010913689

FONTS: Set in **Cosmos** and Curlz

Printed in the United States of America

Long, long ago in a faraway ocean where water was clean and pure and everything was bright and beautiful, there lived a family of clams: Farmer Clam, Mrs. Clam, and their four-year-old son, Sam the Clam.

One day, when Farmer Clam was harvesting his monthly crop of kelp, he saw something strange. The water had turned dark, and the waves thrashed violently. Fish were taking shelter in the caves, and even the fiercest of sharks looked panicked.

"Oh, my, gosh," said Farmer Clam, "it looks like a bad storm! I should go inside to take cover."

By the time Farmer Clam reached his house, the storm was almost upon him. The water was racing so fast that he could hardly close the door behind himself. Inside, it felt peaceful and warm. Mrs. Clam was cooking dinner on the hot springs stove, and the water smelled sweet.

Something is wrong—very, very wrong, thought Farmer Clam.

"It sounds bad out there," said Mrs. Clam.

"Yes, it's terrible," replied Farmer Clam.

"Well, dinner will be ready soon. Tell Sam to wash his hands."

"Oh, no!" yelled Farmer Clam, "I thought Sam was with you. He must still be outside in the storm!"

They both rushed to the window and looked out. It was too late. The storm lifted Sam right off of the ground.

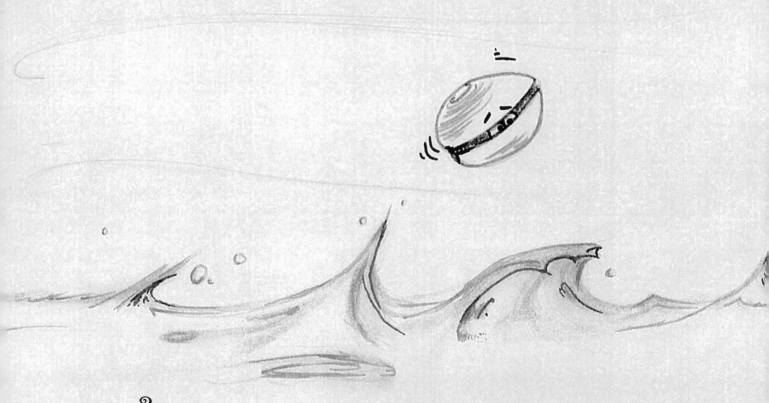

The storm carried Sam for hours. It bounced him across the wave tops and whirled him in countless circles. Sam was scared. There was nothing he could do. Sam closed his shell and cried himself to sleep.

After Sam woke up, he slowly opened his shell to see where the storm had carried him.

"Where am I?" asked Sam. "What kind of a world is this where everything is upside down?"

"It's not everything else, it's you!"

"Yaaah!" screamed Sam. "What are you, and where am I?"

"Well, let me flip you over so you can see."

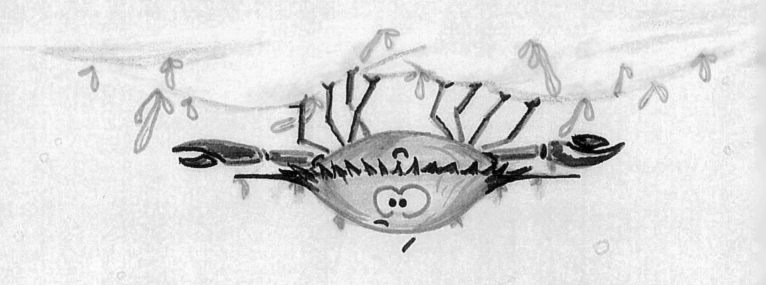

"There. Is that better?"

"Yes, thank you," said Sam.

"You landed on your head when the storm finally dropped you. You are a very young clam. What is your name?" asked the stranger.

"Sam. Sam the Clam," answered Sam.

"Well, nice to meet you, Sam. My name is Jason, and I am a crab."

"I'm afraid that I'm lost, Jason, and I don't know my way home. Do you know where I live?" asked Sam.

"No," answered Jason.

Sam began to cry.

"Don't cry, Sam. You will get home to your family."

"How?" asked Sam.

"I have an old friend who is very wise and who is sure to know where you live. His name is Mike, and he lives in a ship just beyond those hills over there. Would you like me to take you there?"

"Oh, yes!" shouted Sam.

"I'm fine now. Lead the way!"

They arrived at the ship in almost no time because Sam ran all the way. The ship looked very old, and there was a lot of coral and plants growing on it.

"It was a pirate ship," explained Jason. "It has been here for almost two hundred years. It sank after hitting a reef. There was a lot of treasure left on board, but now it belongs to Mike because the ship fell on his house when it sank."

"Are there any guards?" asked Sam.

"Yes, here come some now!" replied Jason.

"What do you want?" asked the guards.
"We need to talk with Mike," answered Jason.
"Tell him that Jason the Crab is here."
"Okay, but wait here," replied one of the guards.

"If you try to enter, you
will be cooked alive!"
"Oh, my," cried Sam.
"We won't move an inch."

Seconds later, the guards returned with Mike. Mike was a large octopus who had jewels around his neck and rings on his arms. After telling Mike his story about the storm, Sam was loaded into a cannon.

"This is surely the way to get you home," said Mike.

"Thank you, Mike and Jason, for being so helpful," said Sam.

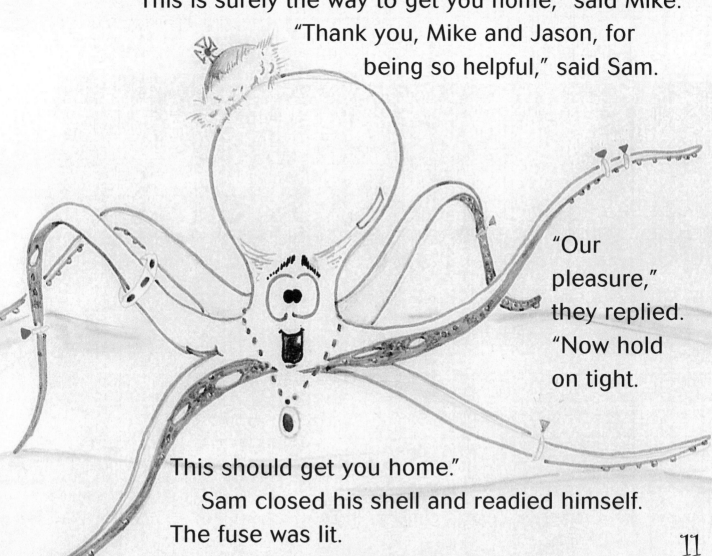

"Our pleasure," they replied. "Now hold on tight.

This should get you home."

Sam closed his shell and readied himself. The fuse was lit.

ZOOM!

The cannon roared, and out shot Sam
faster than any fish had ever swam.
He was on his way home!

Half an hour later Sam finally stopped. He had landed on some rocks, but when he opened his shell he saw he was not at home.

"I will never get home," cried Sam.

It was getting dark, so Sam took out his waterproof matches, made himself a fire, and slowly fell asleep.

Sam woke up to the sound
of screaming squid.
"Run, run for your lives!"
they yelled.
*What is it that is making
them so scared?* thought Sam.

When Sam looked up, he saw what made them scream. It was a great white shark as big as a house, and it swallowed up almost one hundred squid in one gulp.

15

$\mathcal{S}$am did not like the shark eating all the squid, so he sat down to think of a plan. Seconds later, he had an idea!

"Squid, squid! Come here, for I have a plan to rid you of the shark."

The squid gathered around Sam, and he told them his plan.

"If you can persuade the shark to go into that cave over there, I can shut him in forever."

$\mathcal{S}$am swam above the cave to set the trap. He gathered rocks of all sizes and stacked them on top of each other above the entrance of the cave. The trap was set.

"Now squid," yelled Sam,
"get the shark inside the cave!"

The squid gathered together and swam
past the shark and into the cave. The shark
saw the squid and followed them. Soon after
the shark was inside, the squid escaped and
Sam pushed the rocks in front of the cave.

17

From that moment on, the shark was
never seen again.

"Yeah!" cheered the squid. "The shark
is dead. Now we can live in happiness
once again! Thank you for saving us, Sam.
What can we do in return to help you?"

"I'm lost and can't find
my way home," said Sam.

"I live on a kelp farm
with my mom
and dad."

"Well, we
were just going to eat some kelp
for lunch. Maybe it's your dad's place!"
replied the squid.

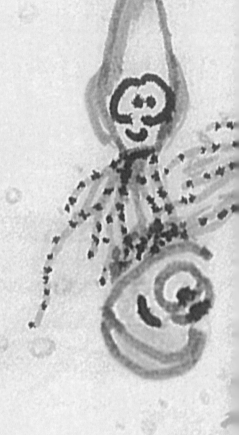

The squid carried Sam
across the sea floor.
"Everything looks very
familiar," said Sam.
"That looks like our farm,
and there's my house with
my mom and dad in front
of it. I'm home!"
Sam was very happy.

19

That night, when his mom and dad tucked him into bed and kissed him good night, Sam told them about his adventures and said, "It's much safer being at home with the people you love."

"Good night. We love you, too, Sam."

After they turned off his light, Sam drifted off to sleep with a smile on his face.

THE END

NATHAN W. LYON wrote "Sam The Clam" at the age of 17 while attending high school at H.B. Woodlawn in Arlington, Virginia. He holds a B.S. in Health Science from James Madison University as well as a Culinary Arts Degree from Le Cordon Bleu.

Young Nathan

Nathan in High School

Nathan's career in television began on the second season of *The Next Food Network Star*, where he finished among the top four. He is the chef and host of *A Lyon in the Kitchen* (Discovery Health and Fit TV) and has appeared as a guest chef/expert on *Home Made Simple* (TLC) and *Real Simple Real Life* (TLC). Nathan is also the cohost, and chef, of *Growing a Greener World* (PBS), and soon, with the help of his family and friends, he will successfully complete his very first cookbook.

Having worked with local growers in California farmers' markets for almost a decade, Nathan believes that good health and education go hand in hand, and that with the help of others, almost anything can be achieved.

Nathan Today

CRAIG A. LYON is Nathan's older brother, and even now, remains bigger than Nathan. Craig was 21 when he illustrated "Sam The Clam." Craig lives with his wife and son in North Carolina, and when he is not writing reports for the pharmaceutical industry, he is a musician, poet, and award-winning playwright.

LaVergne, TN USA
10 December 2010
208238LV00001B